nickelodeon

PIRATE PUPS!

Based on the teleplay "Pups and the Pirate Treasure"
by Ursula Ziegler Sullivan

Illustrated by Fabrizio Petrossi

A GOLDEN BOOK • NEW YORK

T#: 432057

randomhousekids.com

ISBN 978-0-553-53888-5

Printed in the United States of America

20 19 18 17 16 15 14

One day, while exploring the cliffs above
Adventure Bay, Cap'n Turbot slipped and fell down
a dark hole. At the bottom, he discovered an old
pirate hideout.

He was stuck in the creepy cavern, but he knew
who could help him: the PAW Patrol!

Ryder called the PAW Patrol to the Lookout and told them about Cap'n Turbot.

"He's stuck in a cavern filled with pirate stuff, and he thinks it might be the hideout of the legendary Captain Blackfur!" Ryder said. "No one knows what he looked like or what happened to his treasure."

Ryder needed Chase and Rubble for the rescue, but he told the rest of the pups to be ready, just in case.

Rubble was excited. He really wanted to be a pirate!

Ryder, Chase, and Rubble raced to the cliffs and found the hole.

"Chase," Ryder said, "I need your winch hook to lower me into the cave."

"Chase is on the case!" He pulled the hook over, and Ryder locked it onto his safety belt.

Chase carefully lowered Ryder into the dark hole.

The pups joined Ryder and Cap'n Turbot down below. Using Chase's spotlight, they found cool pirate stuff—a spyglass, a flag, and a real pirate hat! Ryder put the hat on Rubble's head.

"*Arr!*" said Rubble. "Shiver me timbers!"

Chase sniffed the air. "I smell seawater," he said. He followed the scent and discovered a secret passage! But it was blocked by rocks.

"That must be the way to the beach," said Ryder.

"Stand back, landlubbers!" said Rubble as he cleared the way with his digger.

Ryder and the pups followed the passage to a beach. They found an old bottle with part of a map inside it.

"Is it a pirate treasure map?" Rubble asked.

"Could be," said Ryder. "We need all paws on deck to solve this mystery."

Ryder called the rest of the pups to the beach and told them that the map had been torn into three pieces.

"There's a clue to where we'll find the next piece," he said. *"'The part of the map that you seek hides in the big parrot's beak.'"*

The pups thought about the clue. Suddenly, Rocky said, "Those boulders at the bottom of Jake's Mountain kind of look like a parrot!"

"Let's check it out," Chase barked.

The team hurried to the rocks that looked like a giant parrot. Skye flew up and found a bottle in its beak. Another piece of the map was inside!

Rocky taped the pieces together, and Ryder read the next clue: *"'From atop Parrot Rock, look toward the sea. A clue hides in the hollow of a very big tree.'"*

"If we can solve that clue," Ryder said, "we should find Blackfur's treasure!"

Chase thought for a moment. "The biggest trees around are in Little Hooty's forest."

"Good thinking!" Ryder exclaimed.

The forest was filled with lots of big trees, so
Chase asked Little Hooty if he had seen an old
bottle in any of the branches. He had!
Little Hooty fluttered up to a hole high in a tree.

Marshall drove his fire
truck to the base of the tree,
extended the ladder, and
climbed up.

"Little Hooty was right!"
he said. He took down a
bottle that contained the last
piece of the map.

Rocky taped the pieces together. They now had the whole map! Ryder read the final clue: *"'Walk twenty paces from the tree toward setting sun and rising sea.'"*

Ryder turned to face the sun and the sea, and he started walking.

From the edge of the cliff, Ryder and the pups saw something amazing through the fog.

It was an old pirate ship next to a deserted island!

"Do you think it's Captain Blackfur's ship?" Rubble asked.

The PAW Patrol worked together to pull the ship onto the beach.

News of the find spread through Adventure Bay. Mayor Goodway and her pet chicken, Chickaletta, came to see the exciting discovery.

On board, Ryder, Cap'n Turbot, and the pups
found an old treasure chest. Inside were coins,
jewels, a gold bone, and even a fancy dog bowl.

"Why would a pirate captain have a dog bowl?"
Marshall asked.

Then, digging through the treasure, Ryder found
an old picture of Captain Blackfur.

Captain Blackfur was a pirate pup!
"He looks just like me, except with a *black fur*
beard!" Rubble exclaimed.
The team let out a mighty *"Arr!"*
Three cheers for the pirate pups of the PAW Patrol!